THE COMPLETE
STAR WARS TRILOGY
SCRAPBOOK

AN OUT-OF-THIS-WORLD GUIDE TO **STAR WARS**,
THE EMPIRE STRIKES BACK, AND **RETURN OF THE JEDI**

Mark Cotta Vaz

SCHOLASTIC INC.

NEW YORK TORONTO LONDON AUCKLAND SYDNEY
MEXICO CITY NEW DELHI HONG KONG BUENOS AIRES

To all kids who love adventure, and especially: Daniel, Matthew, Michael, Katelin, Joseph, and my godchildren, Johnny and Alexandra.

ISBN 0-439-68130-8

TM & ® & © 1997, 2004 Lucasfilm Ltd. All rights reserved. Published by Scholastic Inc.

Book design by Mada Design, Inc.

12 11 10 9 8 7 6 5 4 3 2   4 5 6 7 8 9 1/0

Printed in the U.S.A.
First updated printing, October 2004

May the force be with you

CONTENTS

INTRODUCTION: **BEYOND THE HORIZON**

A long time ago, in a galaxy far, far away there lived a young man named Luke Skywalker. Luke was an orphan who grew up on a moisture farm on the desert planet of Tatooine. Moisture farmers collected and stored every trace of water. With two suns in the Tatooine sky it was always hot and water was precious as gold.

By his eighteenth birthday, Luke had tired of life on Tatooine. He daydreamed about the wonders beyond the horizon. And even though Tatooine was at the frontier edge of the galaxy, Luke knew about the Civil War between the evil Empire and the freedom-loving Rebel Alliance. Luke imagined how glorious it would be to join the Rebels and defeat the Empire.

Then one day a space pod fell out of the sky and landed on Tatooine. Emerging from the pod were two droids named C-3PO and R2-D2. Inside the memory banks of little R2 was a special message for someone called Obi-Wan, who lived alone in the desolate Dune Sea. At Obi-Wan's home they all looked at and listened to a recorded image of Rebel leader Princess Leia. She asked Obi-Wan for help in fighting the Empire.

Obi-Wan told Luke the history of the galaxy. For thousands of years the Old Republic had ruled, with noble Jedi Knights keeping the peace. But years before Luke was born, the Republic collapsed and the Jedi were defeated. Obi-Wan was one of the last of the Jedi Knights. Now the tradition of freedom and justice has been replaced by the Empire's rule of fear and hate.

Obi-Wan revealed that Luke's own father, Anakin Skywalker, had been a Jedi Knight! Obi-Wan had been teacher to Anakin—until the day Darth Vader turned to evil. Now Vader enforced the tyranny of the Empire's leader, Emperor Palpatine.

Obi-Wan asked Luke to leave Tatooine and join him in the fight against the Empire. Luke eventually agreed. Obi-Wan told Luke he would have to learn the ancient Jedi ways and the secrets of the Force. Obi-Wan then gave Luke a lightsaber, the traditional Jedi weapon.

Luke, Obi-Wan, and the two droids went to the spaceport town of Mos Eisley to hire a ship and pilot to fly off Tatooine. They hired a smuggler named Han Solo, commander of the *Millennium Falcon*. Solo boasted that his ship could outrace the mightiest Imperial starship. Also along for the adventure would be Han's loyal copilot, the hairy Wookiee named Chewbacca.

As the *Millennium Falcon* left Tatooine, Luke was excited about his coming adventure. At last he was going beyond the horizon to fulfill his destiny!

THE CIVIL WAR

Around the time Luke was born, the Rebellion against the evil Empire began. The Rebel Alliance soon spread to every star system in the galaxy. The Rebels were great starfighter pilots and very courageous. But the Empire had deadly machines of war and countless soldiers. For lovers of peace and freedom, it was a dark time.

THE EMPIRE

IMPERIAL LEADERS

EMPEROR PALPATINE

The ruthless head of the Empire and ruler of the galaxy. Palpatine had been a young Senator and then the Supreme Chancellor during the twilight of the Old Republic. Many hoped he would restore the Republic to its former glory. Instead he ordered Darth Vader to track down and kill all of the Jedi Knights. With a huge army at his command, Palpatine then directed the construction of the Death Star battle station, the most horrible weapon of destruction ever created.

IMPERIAL ROYAL GUARD

Emperor Palpatine's personal guards, selected from the best Imperial soldiers. Beneath their red robes they wear a suit of armor.

DARTH VADER

The most powerful and feared figure in the galaxy, next to his Master, the Emperor.

GRAND MOFF TARKIN

The Imperial governor in charge of many of the Outer Rim Territories, which include Luke Skywalker's home world of Tatooine. Tarkin, one of the Emperor's closest advisors, oversaw the construction of the first Death Star. Tarkin died in the Battle of Yavin, the first major clash of the Civil War.

THE EMPIRE
FIGHTING SHIPS AND STORMTROOPERS

TIE FIGHTERS

The Empire's main combat starfighters are armed with two laser cannons. Their propulsion and weapon systems are powered by the hexagonal solar panels that extend from each side of the command pod. TIE fighters can't travel great distances, but are launched at specific targets from Star Destroyers or Imperial bases. The TIE pictured here is a TIE Advanced x1 prototype starfighter, custom-built for Darth Vader.

STAR DESTROYERS

These gigantic ships roam the galaxy, spearheading attacks in both deep space and planetary systems. Besides their many built-in turbolasers, a Destroyer can carry whole squadrons of starfighters, ground assault vehicles, and a full division of stormtroopers.

STORMTROOPERS

These fierce soldiers are loyal to the Emperor and the Imperial cause. Here troopers assemble in the main docking bay of the second Death Star (with an Imperial shuttle in the background).

No place in the galaxy is free of the stormtroopers. Below, troopers conduct a search operation.

THE EMPIRE

A group of stormtroopers do a house-to-house search in Mos Eisley, with the help of a probe droid.

SNOWTROOPERS

Snowtroopers are Imperial soldiers trained to operate on the coldest planets. The snowtroopers seen here are accompanying Darth Vader into a captured Rebel base on the ice planet of Hoth.

DEATH STAR

This battle station was the size of a small moon. It was equipped with a superlaser that could destroy an entire planet. Early in the Civil War it destroyed the beautiful planet of Alderaan, the adopted home world of Princess Leia. During the Battle of Yavin that followed, a group of Rebel starfighters attacked the Death Star. Luke Skywalker fired the decisive proton torpedoes that exploded the battle station.

THE SECOND DEATH STAR

After the Battle of Yavin, the Emperor ordered the building of a bigger and more powerful Death Star.

THE EMPIRE

DEATH STAR SHIELD GENERATOR BUNKER

While the second Death Star was being built, it was protected by a force field generated from this station on the forest moon of Endor. Here an Imperial scout trooper prepares to head out on a low-flying speeder bike.

IMPERIAL WALKERS

The All Terrain Armored Transport (AT-AT), or "walkers," are four-legged combat and transport vehicles more than 15 meters tall. Walkers can fire blaster cannons located in the mechanical-head area.

The All Terrain Scout Transport (AT-ST) units are modeled after the larger AT-AT units. The AT-ST units (nicknamed "chicken walkers") can move quickly on their two mechanical legs as well as deliver blaster cannon fire. (Here we see a chicken walker operating near the Death Star shield generator on the forest moon of Endor.)

THE REBEL ALLIANCE
REBEL LEADERS AND HEROES

OBI-WAN KENOBI AND LUKE SKYWALKER

Luke wanted to become a Jedi like his father and asked Obi-Wan to teach him the ways of the Force. And so the great Jedi tradition would continue with this young man who came from a moisture farm on Tatooine.

PRINCESS LEIA ORGANA

A princess and Senator from the planet Alderaan, and one of the greatest leaders of the Rebel Alliance. Before being captured by Vader early in the Civil War, Leia had put stolen plans for the first Death Star into the droid R2's memory banks. This information helped the Rebel starfighters attack and destroy that first battle station. Her efforts to get Obi-Wan to join the Rebellion also led to Luke Skywalker's involvement in the cause. Much later in the Civil War, Luke and Leia would discover an amazing secret: They were twin brother and sister! And Leia, too, had a natural ability to feel the Force.

CHEWBACCA AND HAN SOLO

Chewbacca (or "Chewie"), a fur-covered Wookiee from the jungle planet of Kashyyyk, and Han Solo, a human from the Corellia star system. Solo and Chewie were content to pilot the *Millennium Falcon* on smuggling missions until they met Luke and Obi-Wan, and joined the Rebel struggle against the Empire.

THE REBEL ALLIANCE

MON MOTHMA

As a Senator with the Old Republic, Mon Mothma witnessed the rise to power of Emperor Palpatine and his Empire. Mon Mothma helped organize the galactic-wide Rebel Alliance and was elected leader of the movement.

C-3PO AND R2-D2

The two droids who came to Tatooine with Princess Leia's urgent messages for Obi-Wan and the first Death Star plans. While the gold-colored C-3PO can communicate in speech, R2-D2 speaks in whistles, beeps, and other sounds.

ADMIRAL ACKBAR

A member of the Mon Calamari species and a senior advisor to Mon Mothma. Ackbar helped develop the attack on the second Death Star.

WEDGE ANTILLES

Antilles, a starfighter pilot from the
Corellia star system, fought
alongside Luke Skywalker in the
daring attack on the first Death Star.
Wedge would later lead starfighter
squadrons against the second Death
Star, a fight that would become
known as the Battle of Endor.

NIEN NUNB AND LANDO CALRISSIAN

Nunb (left), from the planet Sullust, served as
copilot to Calrissian during the Battle of Endor.
While Han Solo was involved in the attack on the
forest moon shield generator, Lando piloted the
Millennium Falcon—the ship he once owned but had
lost to Han in a high-stakes card game.

THE REBEL ALLIANCE
FIGHTING SHIPS

X-WING ARMADA

The X-wings are the single-pilot starfighters used by the Rebel Alliance. Here we see a squadron of X-wings in attack formation.

Luke Skywalker pilots his X-wing off of the planet Dagobah.

THE MILLENNIUM FALCON

The *Falcon* was originally a Corellian freighter ship that Han Solo and Chewbacca rebuilt, adding speed and firepower. Here we see the *Falcon* fly over a huge asteroid to escape pursuing Imperial TIE fighters.

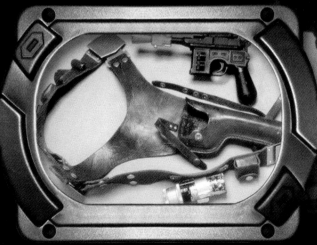

HAN SOLO'S BLASTER AND HOLSTER

Blasters are the main weapons used throughout the galaxy. Blasters deliver bolts of light energy. They can be set from STUN to KILL.

Luke at the controls of one of the *Falcon*'s two turreted laser cannons.

THE REBEL ALLIANCE

REBEL BASES

YAVIN BASE

On the fourth moon of the giant planet Yavin, in thick jungle, are the mysterious temple ruins of a long-lost civilization. The Rebels made this temple their base of operations. From here the Rebels launched their successful strike on the first Death Star.

A rebel guard surveys the jungle and temples surrounding the Yavin base, as the *Falcon* comes in for a landing.

Han Solo prepares to leave the Yavin base hangar.

An X-wing in the Yavin hangar.

HOTH ECHO BASE

Hoth is a world of snow and ice. Here the Alliance converted a giant ice cave into their secret command headquarters, called Echo Base. Unfortunately, the base was discovered by an Imperial force led by Darth Vader. In the resulting Battle of Hoth the Rebels suffered a terrible defeat.

MAIN REBEL BRIEFING ROOM

In this room, located in Admiral Ackbar's personal starship, *Home One*, the Rebellion leadership planned strategy for the Battle of Endor.

SECRETS OF THE FORCE

The ally of a Jedi Knight is the Force, the energy field produced by all living things. The Force flows into a Jedi, allowing him or her to move objects without touching them, to see the future and distant places, and to perform other amazing feats. But there are two sides to the Force: the light and the dark. Jedi Knights, who are in the light, fight only in defense, control their anger, and treat all beings with kindness. But those in the dark are hungry for power and driven by anger, hate, and fear.

THE LIGHT SIDE

JEDI JUSTICE

BEN (OBI-WAN) KENOBI

As a young Jedi Knight, Obi-Wan fought with Luke's father, Anakin Skywalker, in the Clone Wars, the galactic civil war that pitted the Republic versus the Confederacy of Independent Systems (also known as the Separatists). This bloody war lasted years. The Separatists, led by the ex-Jedi Count Dooku, fought primarily with droid armies, while clone troopers defended the Republic.

Obi-Wan was Luke's first great teacher. He taught Luke about the Force, gave Luke his first lightsaber, and led him in training drills. Obi-Wan taught Luke to trust his instinct: "Stretch out with your feelings," he said. Sadly, Darth Vader killed Obi-Wan during a lightsaber duel on the first Death Star. Luke witnessed the death of his friend and teacher moments before he escaped from the battle station.

YODA

The great Jedi Master. It was on the planet Hoth that the spirit of Obi-Wan appeared to Luke in a vision. Obi-Wan told Luke to journey to the planet Dagobah, to continue his training with the Jedi Master Yoda. When Luke arrived on the planet he met a small, green-skinned creature dressed in rags. Luke never suspected this was Yoda! The 900-year-old Yoda had been teaching Jedi Knights, including Obi-Wan, for some 800 years.

LIGHTSABERS

The lightsaber is the special weapon of the Jedi Knight. Inside the handgrip of a lightsaber are power cells and crystals. When activated, a sword-like blade of pure energy appears. A lightsaber blade can cut through almost anything (except another lightsaber blade). During the Civil War the lightsaber was so rare that only Obi-Wan, Vader, and Luke are believed to have used the ancient weapon. Many years of training are required to master the lightsaber. As the final step in his Jedi training, Luke constructed his own lightsaber.

THE LIGHT SIDE

JEDI PHILOSOPHY

Yoda and Luke in Yoda's home.

During his teachings on Dagobah, Yoda explained to Luke how to think like a Jedi Knight.

Sometimes Luke's constant questions frustrated Yoda. "There is no why—clear your mind of questions," Yoda once exclaimed. "Do. Or do not. There is no try."

When Luke asked if the dark side of the Force was stronger than the light, Yoda said no. The dark side, with its anger and hate, was just an easier, more seductive path.

A Jedi Knight must train both mind and body. Here Yoda has Luke keep his physical balance while urging him to make a rock rise in the air using the power of the Force.

While Luke could cause a rock to rise in the air, he didn't believe he could make his X-wing rise out of a muddy lagoon. But to Yoda there was no difference when one embraced the Force. As Luke and R2 looked on, Yoda then used the Force to lift the heavy starfighter out of the swampy water.

Finally, one day, Luke began to feel the Force and through it he had a vision that Leia and Han were in trouble. Luke decided to end his training and leave Dagobah in his X-wing. Yoda, and even the ghost of Obi-Wan, told him of the danger of leaving. Luke was still a student and not yet ready to fight the likes of Darth Vader, they said. Obi-Wan warned Luke he might even be tempted by the dark side. But Luke was fearless and determined to save his friends. He didn't realize he would be stepping into an Imperial trap.

Yoda also knew it was a terrible time for Luke to interrupt his training. "A Jedi's strength flows from the Force, but beware of the dark side," Yoda warned. "Anger, fear, aggression, the dark side of the Force are they. If once you start down the dark path forever will it dominate your destiny."

THE DARK SIDE

Emperor Palpatine was feared throughout the galaxy. He had the Death Star battle stations, the Star Destroyers, and the countless stormtroopers at his command. But few knew the real secret of his power was that he had embraced the dark side of the Force. It was through the Force that Palpatine knew that Luke Skywalker could become a powerful Jedi and threaten his evil rule. During the Galactic Civil War, Palpatine made special efforts to capture Luke and turn him to the dark side.

Darth Vader was also aided by the dark side of the Force. At Emperor Palpatine's command, Darth Vader hunted down and destroyed the Jedi Knights. Vader also held the title "Dark Lord of the Sith." The Sith was an ancient cult that existed thousands of years in the past.

The galaxy is full of crime lords and bounty hunters and the underworld is often called upon to serve the Empire's evil purposes.

One of the most feared crime lords was Jabba the Hutt, who operated his criminal organization from a palace on Tatooine. Han Solo made the mistake of not completing a smuggling job for Jabba. Here Jabba himself confronts Han in the Mos Eisley hangar where Han was storing the *Millennium Falcon*.

Some time after the Battle of Yavin, Vader hired bounty hunters to track down the *Millennium Falcon*, hoping it would lead to the capture of Luke Skywalker. The bounty hunter Boba Fett tracked down the *Falcon* and Luke's friends in the floating Cloud City of Bespin. As a reward, Vader allowed Fett to deliver the captured Han Solo to a vengeful Jabba.

In his ship, *Slave I*, Fett travels the galaxy doing evil deeds for the highest bidder. He is one of the supreme bounty hunters in the galaxy. Boba Fett wears the battle armor of a Mandalorian warrior. His entire suit is a weapon, including wrist lasers and a flame launcher. Fett also wears a jetpack so he can fly short distances.

After delivering Han Solo to Jabba, Boba Fett celebrates with other criminals. Jabba's palace is a noted gathering place for bounty hunters, smugglers, assassins, and other members of the galactic underworld.

THE DARK SIDE

Vader and Obi-Wan clash. During their lightsaber battle Vader boasted that he was now greater than his former Master. But Obi-Wan made this reply: "You can't win, Darth. If you strike me down, I shall become more powerful than you can possibly imagine." Moments later Obi-Wan allowed Vader to kill him, and the great Jedi Master passed on—into the Force.

Darth Vader is greatly feared, because with only a gesture the Sith Lord can kill. Here an Imperial officer has made the fatal mistake of displeasing Vader.

In his vision on Dagobah, Luke saw that his friends were in danger in the floating Cloud City of Bespin. When Luke arrived, Darth Vader was waiting. And even though Luke gave a valiant effort in their lightsaber duel, Vader easily defeated him.

Vader reached out, inviting Luke to experience the dark side. Vader also revealed the secret that Obi-Wan and Yoda had kept from Luke—Darth Vader was Luke's father! Vader told the horrified young man that they could rule the galaxy as father and son. Although Luke managed to escape, he was now confused and troubled. Perhaps it was his destiny to join the dark side. . . .

THE HELMET OF DARTH VADER

Darth Vader had once been known as Anakin Skywalker, a noble Jedi Knight, Clone War hero, and apprentice of Obi-Wan. But Anakin was impatient and took the quick path to the Force by embracing the dark side. Obi-Wan tried to save Anakin but the two fought, and Anakin fell into a molten pit. Anakin survived but he had to wear life-sustaining black body armor and this special breathing helmet. In Obi-Wan's view, when his friend and student embraced the dark side, Anakin Skywalker "died" and Darth Vader was born.

WONDERS OF THE GALAXY

Despite the Civil War, the galaxy was still a place of wonders. Vast star systems were full of planets with varied environments, amazing cultures, and strange creatures. The ability to travel throughout the galaxy at faster-than-light speed was made possible through the discovery of the dimensional corridor, or hyperspace.

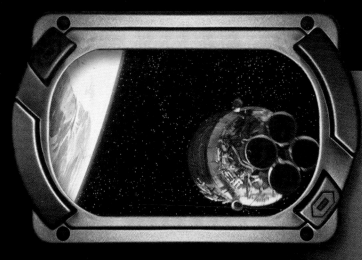

Here we see the escape pod bearing the droids C-3PO and R2-D2 dropping into the Tatooine atmosphere.

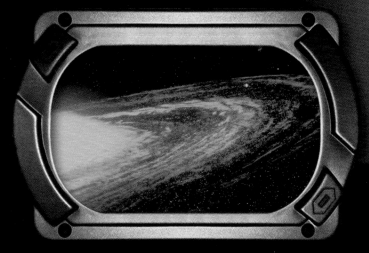

The beauty of star formations spinning like wheels in space.

TATOOINE

Two suns blaze in the sky above the desert world of Tatooine.

There are many ways to travel on Tatooine. Sail barges move across the desert using sails to catch the wind while anti-gravity units propel the craft off the ground.

JABBA THE HUTT'S PALACE

On one of their later trips to Tatooine, the droids joined Luke, Leia, Chewie, and Lando to rescue Han Solo from the crime lord's dark palace.

Landspeeders are another anti-gravity vehicle. Here Luke, Obi-Wan, and the droids pilot their landspeeders into Mos Eisley.

CLOUD CITY

In the Bespin star system, in the cloudy atmosphere above the planet Bespin, is the wondrous floating Cloud City. The city is a famed mining outpost and trading port. Here we see Han Solo and his crew greeted by Lando Calrissian and his aides after having docked the *Millennium Falcon* on a landing pad.

During a card game, Lando won the right to preside over Cloud City. Lando misused this responsibility by betraying Han Solo and allowing Darth Vader to set a trap for the *Millennium Falcon* and its crew. Lando ultimately redeemed himself by joining the fighting forces of the Rebel Alliance, and helping to rescue Han.

EWOK VILLAGE
SANCTUARY MOON OF ENDOR

In the remote star system of Endor, above the planet Endor, is a moon full of forests. In the great trees live the furry little beings known as Ewoks. A typical Ewok village is built around the great tree trunks, with wooden bridges and walkways connecting the forest community. It was near the village pictured here that the Empire built the Death Star shield generator bunker and where the ground attack in the Battle of Endor was waged.

THE WOOKIEE CHEWBACCA

Chewie served as copilot and expert mechanic on the *Millennium Falcon* prior to joining Han Solo in the Rebellion.

Chewbacca's fur-covered body protects him from the cold of Hoth.

Chewie and the droids relax with a strange kind of chess game aboard the *Falcon*.

Chewie, wearing a breathing apparatus, leaves the *Falcon* to investigate a cavern within a huge asteroid. (Chewie and Han discovered they had actually landed inside the mouth of a gigantic space slug. They made their escape moments before the slug closed its huge mouth.)

JAWAS

Jawas are small beings native to the planet Tatooine. They dress in cloaks, glowing eyes visible from beneath their hoods. They travel in a huge, slow vehicle known as a sandcrawler. They are expert scavengers who search the dunes and desert canyons for anything they can fix up and sell. A Jawa is always prepared for the dangers of the desert and will use his blaster if necessary.

JAWA BLASTERS

TUSKEN RAIDERS

Also know as "Sand People," Tusken Raiders are native to Tatooine. They never stay in one place and are constantly moving through the desert land. To survive heat and sand storms they wear heavy robes, eye protectors, and masks. Sand People are very violent. The figure pictured here is waving a gaderffii (or "gaffi stick"), the traditional weapon of his people.

GAFFI STICK

EWOKS

The furry Ewoks of Endor's forest moon are a hunting tribe and can be fierce warriors. Their forest world is sacred to them. For power, many shamans and warriors in a tribe will wear skulls, bones, feathers, and other things found in the forest.

CANTINA CHARACTERS

Obi-Wan once called Mos Eisley a "wretched hive of scum and villainy." The worst place in that dusty Tatooine town is the cantina bar. It's a favorite destination for bounty hunters, smugglers, and criminals throughout the galaxy. Here are some visitors during a typical night at the cantina.

Bib Fortuna

JABBA'S PALACE

Jabba the Hutt and Bib Fortuna. The Hutts are an ambitious species from the planet Varl. Bib Fortuna, a chief lieutenant in Jabba's court, is of the Twi'lek species from the planet Ryloth.

Salacious Crumb, one of the favored members of Jabba's palace court. Crumb is a rare monkey-lizard species that comes from the planet Kowak.

A Rodian and a Jawa visit in Jabba's palace.

DEWBACKS

A giant reptile native to Tatooine, Dewbacks can withstand high desert temperatures and are ideal as beasts of burden or for riding long distances.

BANTHAS

These fur-covered creatures are as big as elephants. Banthas are used as beasts of burden. On Tatooine, banthas are prized among the Tusken Raiders, who are said to have a special bond with the animal.

CREATURES

RANCOR BEAST

Until recently, it was believed that this giant rancor was the only such creature in existence. For the amusement of Jabba the Hutt, this rancor was kept in a special pit in his palace. During the mission to rescue Han Solo from Jabba's clutches, Luke battled and killed the monster.

TAUNTAUNS

Tauntauns are found on the frozen wastelands of Hoth. They usually travel in herds, their thick fur protecting them from extreme cold. When the Rebels had their base on Hoth, tauntauns were valuable as pack animals and for short trips outside Echo Base.

Han and Luke survey the frozen land.

WAMPA ICE CAVE

Except for the tauntauns, few other life forms are known to exist on Hoth. One known creature is the flesh-eating, white-furred wampa. Using their powerful claws, these creatures can carve out their own ice caves. With their white fur they blend into the snow, which is how one wampa surprised and captured Luke. The wampa took Luke to its cave and hung him upside down. Using the Force, Luke managed to escape this terrible place.

THE SARLACC

The Sarlacc lives in a sand pit in Tatooine's Dune Sea. You can see the open mouth of this fearsome creature at the bottom of the pit. When Jabba the Hutt captured Luke and his friends, he was planning to feed them to the Sarlacc. But Luke Skywalker—now mature and advanced in his Jedi training—saved the day.

DROIDS

C-3PO

There are different types of droids. C-3PO, for example, is a protocol droid and can speak more than six million languages.

R2-D2

R2 is an astromech droid. These droids specialize in spaceship repair, maintenance, and navigation. R2 flew with Luke in his X-wing during the Battle of Yavin and also accompanied him to Dagobah. R2 played a vital role in the early part of the Civil War, because Princess Leia stored the first Death Star plans in R2's memory banks.

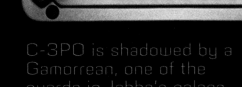

C-3PO is shadowed by a Gamorrean, one of the guards in Jabba's palace.

R2-D2 gets muddy in the swamp world of Dagobah.

PROBE DROID

Also called probots, these flying machines are equipped to gather and transmit information. This Imperial probe droid discovered the existence of the Rebel base on Hoth, which led to the invasion by Darth Vader's forces.

MEDICAL DROID

When Luke was rescued from the wampa ice cave he was near death from exposure to the freezing cold. Back at Echo Base, he was saved with a session in this special tank—and by the attention of medical droid 2-1B.

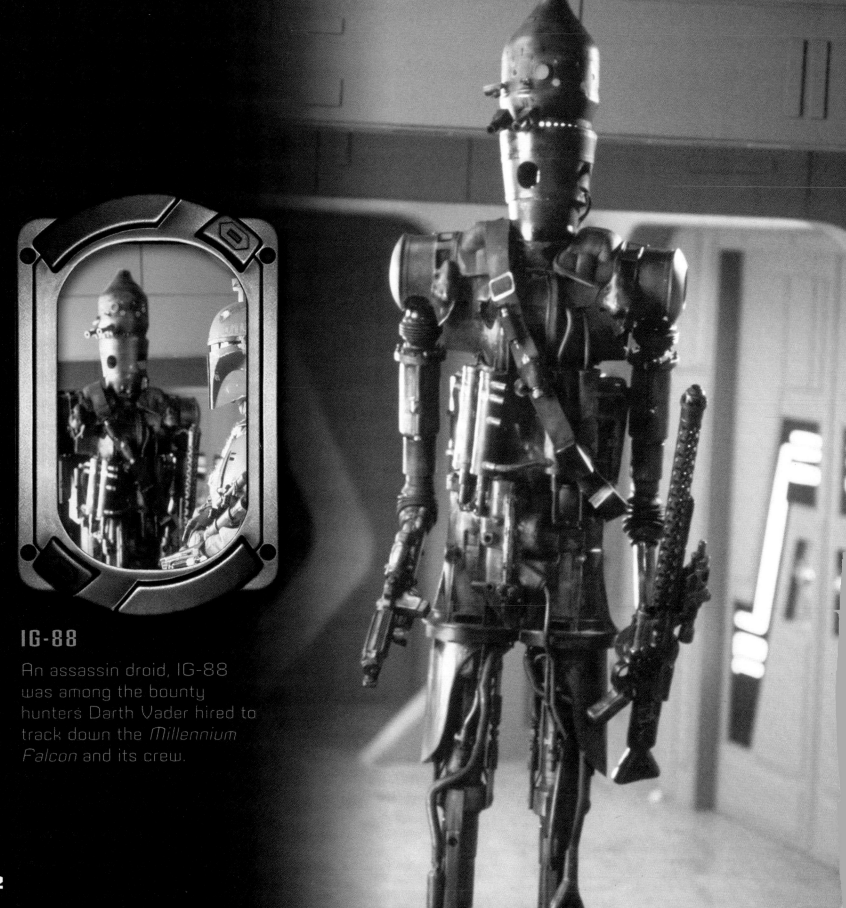

IG-88

An assassin droid, IG-88 was among the bounty hunters Darth Vader hired to track down the *Millennium Falcon* and its crew.

FAMOUS BATTLES

The Galactic Civil War began before the Battle
of Yavin and ended with the Battle of Endor.

BATTLE OF YAVIN

This battle was one of the first major events of the Civil War and a stunning victory for the Rebel Alliance. The battle was named after the planet Yavin, from whose moon the Rebels launched their attack on the first Death Star. Thanks to the stolen Death Star plans the Rebels had learned of a weakness in the battle station. But victory was still a long shot: A starfighter would have to fly down a trench in the Death Star and score a direct hit through an open exhaust vent to explode the power core.

To get to the Death Star exhaust vent, the attacking X-wings had to escape chasing TIE fighters—including Darth Vader's own TIE Advanced x1. Luke Skywalker was flying down the trench when he heard Obi-Wan's voice telling him: "Use the Force, Luke!" Luke trusted the Force, fired his laser torpedoes, and escaped just as the Death Star exploded.

After the Battle of Yavin, a special ceremony was held in the throne room of the Yavin moon temple. The heroes Luke Skywalker, Han Solo, and Chewbacca ascend the throne room steps to be honored by Princess Leia before this festive gathering of the Alliance.

While the Battle of Yavin was the first great victory for the Rebellion, the Battle of Hoth was a decisive Imperial victory. Here Rebel troops in frozen ice trenches await the invasion force.

The Imperial attack was led by the giant mechanical walkers.

BATTLE OF **HOTH**

Direct hits from the walkers cause the Rebel troops to scatter.

Walkers advance as Rebels retreat. Luckily many of the heroes of the Rebellion managed to escape. The Alliance would regroup and plot their final attack on the new Death Star being constructed.

While Lando Calrissian piloted the *Millennium Falcon* during the direct attack on the second Death Star, Han Solo and Leia went to the forest moon of Endor to strike against the protective shield generator. Here a scout trooper races a speeder bike through the nearby forest, chased by Leia.

Destroying the protective shield generator was the key to the Death Star attack. Here the Empire made a fatal mistake by thinking the Ewoks, with their primitive weapons, were not a threat. But the Ewoks joined forces with Han Solo's group and together they destroyed the generator. With the shield down, Lando, Wedge, and other Rebel starfighters could successfully attack the Death Star (which had just become operational). Lando flew the *Millennium Falcon* and fired the missiles that exploded the Death Star.

THE FINAL BATTLE
LUKE REVEALS HIS JEDI POWERS

When Darth Vader first defeated Luke, the young man still had much to learn about the ways of a Jedi. Here we see him confident and sure of his powers as he faces Jabba the Hutt's men. Luke has become a true Jedi Knight.

With a slash of his lightsaber, Luke stops Boba Fett.

LUKE DEFEATS DARTH VADER

The final lightsaber battle between Luke and Vader was held in the sight of Emperor Palpatine in the throne room on the second Death Star. Luke tried to avoid the fight, and only struck back in self-defense. Luke ultimately defeated his father, but refused to kill him. He believed there was still good in his father. "Let go of your hate," Luke told him, even as the Emperor ordered Luke to embrace hate and join the dark side.

When the Emperor attacked Luke, Vader turned on his Master to save his son. In their struggle the Emperor was killed and Vader fatally wounded. Luke went to Vader's side and removed the black helmet so they could gaze into each other's eyes. "You were right about me," Luke's father said with his dying breath, admitting that Luke had seen the spark of goodness that had been buried within him for so many years. Luke escaped with Vader's armor just as the Death Star exploded. Luke honored Anakin Skywalker with a hero's funeral pyre on the forest-moon of Endor.

After the Rebel victory at the Battle of Endor, our heroes celebrate on the forest moon: The droids C-3PO and R2-D2, Han Solo, Princess Leia, Luke Skywalker, and Chewbacca. This triumph for the Alliance ended the Galactic Civil War.

The Rebel celebration went on deep into the night. At one point Luke gazed out into the dark forest and saw an amazing sight: Anakin Skywalker, Obi-Wan, and Yoda (who had recently passed away), smiling and looking at him with pride. Luke smiled back, knowing his father and teachers would always be looking out for him, guiding him from beyond—at one with the Force.

EPILOGUE: **A NEW HOPE**

For Luke Skywalker, the Civil War had not only been a victory against the evil Empire, but a personal triumph. He had been taught by the great Jedi Obi-Wan and Yoda, made a lifelong friend in Han Solo, became reunited with his twin sister, Leia, and forged a final peace with his father. Ahead of him lay new adventures and new explorations of the wondrous galaxy.

THE FORCE WILL BE WITH YOU —ALWAYS!